what arrives after treefall

what arrives after treefall

to theodore theodore,

my greatest love and
inspiration. you are a
dog I would do any-
thing for

table of contents

preface

My first novel, *Lost in the Garden*, sits poorly formatted on my shelf. Its binding is in hardcover, yet it's only a first draft. I intended to edit it when I was a freshman, but now I can't even force myself to read it. It was an exploration of Jewishness and queerness, a contemporary novel written during a time when I learned more about myself than I ever wanted.

That was only the first of several novels, and my tastes have shifted, though not wholly changed, since. With over 868,000 words written from 2018 to 2020 alone, I'd be surprised if my tastes didn't grow with me.

I've found myself drawn to the same four things every time I sit down to draft: extra bones, chronic pain, sapphicness, and making the gore as beautiful as roses. Even when I don't intend for a story's narrative to talk about extra bones, the main characters always end up with pain in their feet. I've thought carefully about the sources of their pain and mine; my accessory navicular bones in my feet are rare, and my chronic pain syndrome even rarer. Writing about these conditions is both an outlet and a way to share my experience with others.

I've settled on calling my sexuality "sapphic," referring to same-gender attraction between women in the past year. Because of this, more often than not, my works have an f/f relationship in the spotlight. Many of the pieces you'll find in this anthology share the same fate. I have found that I love the quiet moments between characters, even amid a gory narrative. This anthology doesn't shy away from carnivorous deer and murder, but it does give those scenes the same level of lure as descriptions of sapphic love, nature, and divine beings.

What Arrives After Treefall centers on two themes: nature and abandonment. The latter I didn't intend to write, but all the pieces I considered for publication had emotional or physical abandonment. Since November 2020, I have been struggling with fears of abandonment and the reality of it. If I use "abandonment" loosely, then I've been dealing with abandonment in some way since my house burned down in November 2012. Losing places, losing people, losing animals—losing what I care about has impacted me deeply. I have come past it to the point where I can write about characters struggling with the same things as me, though I foresee myself working through abandonment in the far future. I use abandonment as a theme in this anthology loosely, as I consider abandoned corpses and cottages to suit the theme well enough. Abandonment by people and abandoning non-tangible things can also be found in this anthology.

The other theme, nature, is born of my love for the outdoors and aesthetics. I traveled and hiked frequently growing up, so I draw from my experiences with every piece. My descriptions of forests, especially, are reminders of the life I want to forge for myself. During my weekly hikes in middle school, I basked in the heat of Southern California until my feet would hold up no longer. In recent years, I've traveled across the country and Europe and found a home among towering trees and icy rivers. Scotland, my ancestor's home, and Belgium, my stepbrothers' homeland, both welcome overgrown ruins and old homes as a part of their natural landscape. My clan's castle is slowly being reclaimed by the ocean and rolling hills of Mull. I long to spend more time in these places—places where the natural and old artificial landscapes coalesce into a single space. My love of the beauty of nature is reflected in my anthology, in which almost every piece is an ode to the natural environment.

When I first came to SDSCPA, I would have never guessed how much I ended up growing as a writer here. I learned how to collaborate with others, attended several workshops across the nation, won YoungArts and Scholastic Art & Writing, and found writers I'll be in contact with for years to come.

Above all else, this anthology was written for my freshman self—the nervous girl who didn't know who she'd become or what she'd create. As the years went on, I pushed myself to create and create and create until I arrived at this anthology. *Lost in the Garden* was the only first step of a tall staircase.

follow the forest

she weaves through the forest
    a sword on her back, axe in between her palms
over fallen logs and pebbles in streams

the forest—alive, never empty—
a girl in shining armor—free, ever watchful—

she recoils at a scream, reacting and wary
the forest prods at edges of her mind

she is surrounded
    by trees and birds, ferns and lizards
skitters and pauses. waits for the last toad's croak

she dips her fingers in the river
    led through the shallows
the forest shivers as her axe drags through bubbling waters
    it cries as shedding leaves

but when the road splits,
and a monster roars

                                               i.
she unsheathes her sword and steps over skeletons
finds the monsters hiding.
    are they weak?
are they scared? are they waiting?

follow, find the cracks in their scales, plates,
armor. bleed one. let them cry—

the forest shields her as the sky sheds water like
    snakes shed skin
she takes the hand of the maiden,
safe and quiet the world became

                                               ii.
she finds herself between two creatures
flanked, scared, weak. claws sink into soft dirt
    tears apart her skin

through armor and nails, the monsters dig into her
    and abandon her body under leaves

    puckered and sored
the forest engulfs her in its roots
no maiden waits at the end of this journey

sword and axe drop

below the greenhouse

A beast hunted me through a forest, waiting for my muscles to burn and give out. Blood dripped down its jawbones as its immense weight crunched everything beneath it.

Lose it, I told myself. *Lose it and win.*

I pulled my cap down as I bolted. The forest surrounded me in a blaze of greenery. Any other day, I'd trail my fingers among dew-laden leaves and flowers. But today, I reached for my rifle strap and compass. Sweat dripped past my brow. No matter what—no matter how lost I got—I refused to lose this fight.

I risked a glance back at the beast chasing me. It lept between trunks like any other resident of the forest yet it lacked the skin of its neighbors. The blood. The life. It was built of bones and magic, older and wilder than any place outside this forest could offer.

And its bones and magic taught me why I should be wary of the forest's edge. I'd only been stationed in Marillis for a few weeks and no townsfolk explained their fear. They stayed in their clearing, hiding as my partner, Nathaniel, and I patrolled Marillis's outskirts. They ran when the beast greeted us with teeth tearing into Nathaniel's flesh.

I winced as branches tore through my shirt and into my skin. How the beast survived while rocks scratched its bones, I was far from the one to know.

A north-facing trail stretched across the forest floor—the first path I've seen since passing the woodland edge. With its sparseness, it almost blended in with the soil and grass. I ran alongside it, praying it would lead somewhere the beast couldn't reach.

The path led down a steep slope to a river, rocky and sharp. Various small waterfalls spread across its width—their bubbling covered my panting breath as I drew near. I focused only on the reformed path as rapids hit my torso and soaked my woolen coat and rucksack with cold water. Raised high above my head, my rifle avoided splashes by inches. As soon as I reached the shore, I dragged myself out by gripping weeds.

I lifted the rifle to my shoulder and squeezed the trigger while the beast first entered the river—splashing, watching. A bullet embedded itself in its skull. It didn't falter.

I scampered up the slope until the north-facing path met one leading west, both deeply hidden by tall grass. I wove between boulders and patches of nettles until a circular building reflected morning light a couple hundred meters away.

I needed to make it out alive. I needed to win.

#

My hands shook as the door screeched open. My stomach dropped. The building seemed to be a grand greenhouse, two stories in height, but plants grew to the height of the ceiling—even beyond, poking through glass. This disorganized scenery offered no protection, but I could still hide.

I stepped inside, weaving between pots of seedlings and buckets of water. The back of the greenhouse was out of sight, hidden by foliage.

"Drop your weapon," a voice said. I spun

16

around to face a woman whose shovel pointed at me accusingly. "What are you doing here?"

I put my hand up as I set the rifle on the ground. My fingers left its wood clammy. "I'm being chased."

"By what?"

"By a beast."

The woman lowered her shovel. "No beasts live in these woods any longer. It's empty but for me—"

The beast roared outside, close enough for my skin to prickle.

She set the shovel aside and ducked under a thick layer of plants. I followed her lead.

"You should've let it take you."

I recoiled. She knew about the beast—she lied. "I don't want to die like that."

"Neither do I." The woman dug through her skirt pockets until she pulled out a scrap of fabric. "Tell me, why did you come so far into the woods?"

As she spoke, I quickly clambered for my rifle and its comforting weight before returning to the safety of the plants. No need to be exposed for long. I aimed toward the door. "Before my partner died, we were meant to protect the village. I don't run when things go wrong."

"So you'd rather kill me instead?"

"Absolutely. Us over many? It's always the better choice. " I sunk closer to the ground, hidden from the entrance by a grand leaf, and offered her my hand. "I'm Greer."

"Addifer." She refused, tucking her arm behind her. "This beast you speak of is the Monster. It'd devour all of Marillis in a matter of hours, so be thankful you didn't take it there." She dropped her voice, barely a whisper. "Now, be quiet. Though it may not see, the Monster listens."

Branches snapped underfoot. Its bony body ground against itself, barely bound together by rotting sinew. Mossy antlers rose out of its canine-like skull, and hooves pounded against the ground with every step.

"If it comes closer, I'm running," I said.

"It won't enter." Addifer crawled to a tray of potted flowers. Tight-

17

ening the straps of her gloves, she tore a bud off the stem before wrapping it in a scrap of fabric. Its salmon-colored petals spread out like a fan. She paused when my expression faded into distaste. "Death follows the Monster, and now it follows you."

I tossed her a knife from my rucksack. "Flowers and shovels won't protect you when the Monster comes."

The knife clattered against the ground. "Hm, somehow I'm still alive."

"When did you meet it?" I asked.

"Humans don't come around here, Greer."

The sound of the Monster's antlers against glass rattled throughout the greenhouse.

I took Addifer's wrist and broke out into a sprint toward the greenhouse's entrance. She attempted to pull away, but I was stronger. It would rip her apart like it did Nathaniel. I wasn't risking that.

"It's my duty to protect you," I said. "You may not live in Marillis, but you're not dying while I'm around."

"Then you're headed in the wrong direction." She used my grip against me to pivot deeper into the mess of plants. They curved a tunnel above our heads, leaves drooping like willow. Addifer focused straight ahead—she led me through twists and turns, between pots and cages of plants. I reached out to touch a few of them, but she pulled my hand back. "They're poisonous."

I pressed my arms close to my body until we reached her house. It lay in the center of the greenhouse, built of sturdy oak with a curved roof and vines snaking up walls.

"Did you build this yourself?" I looked her slender body up and down. That question didn't make sense. "Why here?"

"The Monster was trapped here. The greenhouse was a byproduct—another layer of protection for the rest of the world." Addifer stopped. She fidgeted with her sleeve. "Be thankful you found this place. The Monster is too afraid to enter."

"But we can try," I said.

"My family did, too, but now they're dead."

We're trapped as much as it was.

18

#

Inside, she sat at a table and unwrapped a bright pink flower. Though she still wore gloves, she touched the flower as little as possible as she crushed it in a bowl. I sat across from her, but my eyes wandered. Most surfaces were covered with plants or dusty memorabilia. Corners held cobwebs, but no spiders.

"Do you have any food?"

I blinked. My rucksack held a few rations. I gave her jerky.

My attention wandered again, refocusing on a painting of a family hung on the wall across me. A black-haired woman and a brunet rested their hands on the shoulders of four girls. I recognized the smallest as Addifer from her gloves and black braid. The rest had their throats ripped, revealing bleeding canvas. I frowned. That clashed with the painting's elegance.

Addifer noticed my expression. "What? Does death make you uncomfortable?"

"Can't say I've had much experience." My first deployment—a quiet town—would've been a fine place to live for a few years with a friend like Nathaniel. I thought I got lucky.

"The Monster took my family away from me. Thanks to you, it might finally end me."

I didn't know how to respond, so I walked around instead. Behind me, there were steps leading downstairs. The ones for upstairs were closer to Addifer, so I kept away. She was deep in focus, rolling the flower paste and jerky into a ball. She wrapped it in fabric.

I only got through the door frame before Addifer ripped me back.

"Don't even try." Her fingers dug into my collarbone.

"Okay, okay. I won't." I put my hands up in defeat and sat on the ground. "I'm sorry."

She ignored me in favor of leaving the house with a basket in hand. I groaned into my palms. The only person I could possibly talk to and I insulted her.

I pinched the bridge of my nose—I had to follow her. I stepped outside as she turned the corner of the house. The trail I walked on was well-worn, leading to a garden behind the house. Vegetables grew in planters, but no Addifer.

Something rustled a dozen meters away behind overgrown weeds, too small to hide the Monster but large enough for a person.

"Addifer?" I crept closer.

She crouched beside a cellar and pressed shovels against her palm. They left red welts.

Chuckling, I said, "If my rifle barely makes a dent against the Monster, a shovel won't do anything."

Shrugging, she tried another. Its tip left a bead of red on her skin. "If worse comes to worst, something will have to protect me. I'm not going without a fight."

The sharpest shovel went into her skirt pocket and a parcel of paste came out. She called the contents oleander. "We might need this. If not for the Monster, then for us. It'll be less painful than the alternative."

Oh, poison.

#

We ate tomatoes on the floor of her house. Addifer cut into them with a knife and fork, while I bit right into them. By the time I tried to start up a conversation, we'd eaten the majority of tomatoes.

"How far are we from Marillis?"

"At least six miles, if not farther. I don't make a habit to be close enough to know," she said. "Unfortunately, the forest between us and the town is the Monster's domain."

That was a relief. "Ah. It doesn't venture out, then."

She sliced up her fourth tomato. "Not often, though it might if we don't give it what it wants. Then again, it's just eaten, so no promises." Her head ducked down as the glass reverberated again. Still no shattering, still safe. "Actually, it might feast soon, but you'll likely survive. Pray everyone else does, too."

I rested my head on my knees and took a deep breath. I was a soldier, stationed in Marillis to protect and support them. I wasn't doing that by loitering around here with Addifer.

That could change, though. As soon as Addifer turned her back, I could give the Monster what it wanted. She'd no longer be bothered by me.

"How long ago did they die?"

Her cutting stopped. "A few years ago."

She wrapped leftover tomatoes in fabric and waited by the side door. "I'll be back in just a moment—I have a few more vegetables to pick."

"Don't get eaten," I said half-jokingly.

"Not planning on it."

She closed the door with a smile.

#

I took off my coat and rucksack—it's clear I'd be here for a while. And so I sought out entertainment. Addifer's house was three stories tall, the uppermost level dedicated to something unknown and the lower something sinister. I couldn't tell what, but the way Addifer pushed me away from it meant it was anything but good.

The upper was where I began my search.

A flight of stairs led to a bedroom with even more plants. This time, most were small enough to fit in my palm. I held the smallest of saplings in its painted pot. It's obvious Addifer adored her plants.

While the house downstairs was barren of interest—mostly practical things like utensils and watering cans—this room was a home. Countless pots and paints perched on shelves, their colors matching the variation on plants outside.

I stared for a time until a crash sounded from outside. Setting down the pot, I rushed downstairs and grasped my rifle. She wasn't back yet.

"Addifer? Are you okay?" I called.

The vegetable garden lay empty except for her tomato basket.

I ran from toward the entrance of the greenhouse, seeking the areas where plants thinned and paths formed. My toes caught on rocks, and I stumbled, but I kept moving.

When I got close to the greenhouse's door, I slowed. For what I wanted, I had to be patient. I crept through the doorway and behind a nearby bush. All I heard was the Monster's movements.

I eyed it through foliage. I rested on my toes, steadying myself with nearby branches. Through the leaves, I noticed glimpses of cream-colored bones.

21

Underbrush crunched beneath its paws, pacing the distance between the meadow and riverbed. Addifer stood strong with her shovel aimed at its spine. She panted. This fight would end with one feasting on the other if I didn't get involved.

I shot the floor beneath its hooves. Not enough to hurt it, but that wasn't my intention. I wanted to be loud.

"Miss me?"

I ran perpendicular to its charge. Addifer was only a few steps away—but she wasn't dying so quickly. I pulled her by her shoulder to the greenhouse's entrance, slamming the door shut behind us. Glass rattled.

She collapsed in my arms and pressed her face into my chest. "Greer, you shouldn't have done that. I was handling it."

"Getting yourself killed isn't 'handling it.'"

"If I'm the one person it couldn't get to, then I'm the person it wanted most," she said. She choked up on the last words. "Then this... Everything could be over. You wouldn't have to worry about Marillis anymore."

"I may have just met you, I'm not abandoning you so easily."

I looked up from her to see the Monster looming over the doorway. Its antlers poked at already weak panes, hooves scratched the exterior. I pushed Addifer away as forcefully as I could. It wanted someone to eat, here I was.

Glass shattered into thousands of fragments, many as large as steak knives. I sliced down my palm with one. I drew its attention toward me—like sharks, it sought out fresh blood.

"Come and get me."

I applied pressure as I ran through the densest areas of the greenhouse, weaving between vines. They whacked the Monster with loud slaps and alerted me to its location.

This wasn't just about me.

My gait got rougher with every step, crossing mismatched distances over roots and leaves. Though I used plants as cover, the greenhouse's size wouldn't keep it away for long. Only a few moments until it got a step ahead.

I jumped for a burning lantern—fueled by candles, no doubt—and blew it out. Its frame hit the Monster's face, a chain lashing into the eye socket, then slithering out. The Monster pawed the crushed remains of the lantern—bewildered. My breathing shallowed.

"You're afraid, huh?"

Running again, I made a sharp turn when the pots and roots got thicker. The Monster lumbered along behind me, snapping stems. A little longer. Enough for Addifer to escape.

The path interlaced with plant life ready to hinder me. My feet landed at awkward angles. While I ducked under every branch, the Monster ran straight through. Plants toppled behind it, but we were almost there.

Raised garden beds were the first hint of what to come. They offered tomatoes and carrots—nothing to help me against an impenetrable beast. I cleared the distance before the Monster could realize my plan.

Beside the weeds, I found shovels too dull to draw blood, but their poles reached my hip. I held one, blood dripping down the handle, and turned to face the Monster again.

It lunged.

The Monster's hooves hit my chest as soon as the shovel clanged against its head with a hearty swing. It lurched forward while I turned out of the way, hitting the wooden doors of the cellar. They shattered.

I fell, my soft body slapping the ground before the Monster crunched.

#

I lay there, flat against the rocky floor. The distance I fell wasn't far—two stories up at most—but the ache and breathlessness overwhelmed me. Addifer had said something about trapping it, but this? Nothing I could have guessed. Not within the confines of the greenhouse.

The Monster's head lay low, weighed down by its own skull. One of its legs was shattered, but even dogs could survive with three. This wasn't going to save me.

Sitting up, I noticed the walls covered in white scratches, almost overtaking the cellar entirely.

Caged, the Monster roared.

I steadied my rifle to point directly into its eye sockets. They were empty and cracked, like the dead deer I stumbled across as a kid.

"I—I'll kill you if you try to do anything." My voice cracked.

It brought its hooves closer to its chest, unafraid of my childish threats.

"I swear. Please... *Please* leave me alone. I can feed you. There's plenty in the woods I could hunt, so you can rest." I took the parcel of oleander out of my pocket. The fabric it was wrapped came slightly undone. The meat held. "See? I have more, I promise."

The Monster caught the parcel in its great maws, gnawing on the tough fabric.

I swung my rifle behind my back. A few moments longer.

"If you let me go for a moment, I promise—swear on my life—I'll come back. I'll feed you more."

I slid backward until I pressed against a wooden door, made with the promise of protection. As I raced to take hold of the handle, the Monster stood and loomed over my head. I covered my clammy hands with my sleeve to briefly open it.

The Monster rammed its deerlike antlers into the door as soon as it closed, barely missing me. Safe and alone, I took a deep breath and immediately gagged. Rotting flesh congealed with decade-old rat feces in an underground room—I knew who died here.

I wanted to vomit. I couldn't stop panting and sucking in deep gulps of air. As long as the door didn't splinter, I had survived the Monster. I won.

My eyes adjusted to the low light slowly, but soon I saw the skeletons of Addifer's family, picked clean by rats. Scattered about the room were their gnawed and shattered bones, drilled deep with bite marks. I covered my mouth. This was—

I pressed my back against wood. The door held.

This was slaughter.

I paused for a few moments before crawling in the vague direction of the exit. It almost blended in with the shadows, if not for the faint light coming from the top of the staircase. I didn't make it halfway before having to sit and steady myself among the feces.

Nothing—not my training, not my family, not my friends—could have prepared me for this day. Nathaniel was gone, Addifer's family long dead, but no one else in Marillis had to suffer at the hands of the Monster.

I pulled myself up the stairs to the door. On the other side, I'd be safe.

#

Addifer found me after a few minutes. Her hair plastered to her forehead and cheeks. Her eyes were wide open, gloved hands holding the same type of fabric the poison was once in.

"Are you okay?" She sat next to me on the steps. The bottom was dark and held a beast who terrified me, but I couldn't bring myself to leave.

I leaned on her shoulder. "Eventually." My palm stung; it didn't bleed much anymore.

She turned my face toward her, forcing me to look her in the eye. "I know what you saw down there wasn't okay. So, tell me the truth."

"I don't know. Maybe?" I pried her fingers off me. "I didn't want to leave you with a lie and guilt. And seeing dead bodies is far better than being too dead to see at all."

I stood and offered her my hand. She took it, so I lifted her up. "Soon, this greenhouse will be safe again."

#

The cellar doors were now made up of broken planks, splintering my fingers as I looked over the edge. The Monster roared, though now I saw how weak it had become. It didn't jump or beg. It watched. Its fate was decided as soon as it had ripped into Nathaniel, and I would make the most of it.

I aimed at the Monster and shot.

#

The next day arrived with brushing broken glass outside the greenhouse, where it'd be safe from anyone stepping on it for the time being. My arms ached with the tug of bandages as I did so, and my injured hand rested in my pocket.

By the time we finished sweeping, the day was far from over. I collected petals of oleander and tossed them into the cellar for the Monster to feed on, while Addifer rinsed my bloody clothes in the river.

We reconvened on the slopes of the river. The midday sun dried my coat and pants as I laid next to her. She curled away from me, her hair spread out around her. Her breathing slowed as she relaxed.

As the sun traveled into the afternoon, we lay there—not speaking, not looking. The weight of the day pressed on my chest while grass tickled my fingers. One dead, two alive, one festering underground. I'd be long gone by the time it hunted again.

Addifer turned toward me and mumbled. Clearing her throat, she said again, "I'm leaving and not coming back. This may be my home, but death lingers here now. I won't stay only to stumble and be the Monster's first meal in weeks, if not years. But…"

"But?" I reached for her face and rubbed a strand of hair between my finger and thumb.

"What about my greenhouse? I can't abandon it—it's the only thing I have left. It's the only thing I've ever really *had*. And—and to think the Monster crushed it so easily just—"

"Shh." I squeezed her hand. "Breathe."

"This Monster ruined my life. It trapped me in here, isolating me from the world and taking away my family. Marillis knows me only as a folk tale, and if I go there and they stare, I wouldn't know what to do anymore. And to think I hid in here like a coward while the Monster plucked off its young. If I hadn't been such a coward and went through with this plan years ago, I could've prevented plenty of avoidable deaths."

"But you caught it. Your choice to run outside and sacrifice it led to me falling into the cellar. They'll remember us both for today, not necessarily the past. This will be a blip in their memory when they realize there's nothing more to be afraid of." Sitting up, I swung my rucksack into my lap. "We can tell them what you've done and then you never have to see them again."

"Where can I go? Because once they know, I'll never be allowed to return to my greenhouse. They'll think I'm helping it escape."

I dug into my rucksack once again; this time, I had a folded scrap of paper. Addifer tilted her head as she unfurled it.

"If we're six miles from Marillis, we're about here." I pointed at an unmarked part of the map. "There's a road right on the forest's edge that'll take us into Marillis and beyond. Where it ends, the Monster is nothing but a folk tale," I said. "Growing up, I never heard it. Chances are, no one will know of you either."

"Could we even make it that far? You're hurt."

I stretched my fingers. "I'll see a doctor in Marillis—I have to stay for a funeral, anyway. A little longer won't hurt." Nathaniel's body hardly looked human. Plus, with the wariness of the townsfolk, I'll be the one to carry his body back.

I looked over at her—her eyes were red and puffy. "Will death still follow me now that the Monster is trapped?" I asked.

She wiped her eyes and half-smiled. "I hope not. I mean, I'm not planning on dying anytime soon."

"Then let's go—there's nothing stopping you from remaking your life. There'll be a greenhouse waiting for you at the other end," I said. "I'll even help you build it."

She helped me up, letting me use her as support. I thanked her for it and held her hand tighter. She smiled at me. This gardener and her oleander.

a quiet paradise

A breeze drifts through the willow's leaves
Rustling your skirts, making you pull ever-closer to my restless heart
This afternoon, a quiet day hiding away from the spring sun
This afternoon, quiet hours spent weaving daisy chains between the
     roots of a willow tree
This afternoon I spend with you
With no one but the gleam of sun on a lazy stream to interrupt us

You are the willow's leaves dipped inches beneath the water's surface
Loved by the waterfall we call our world
Yet, after all our journeys
All the green fields you've called home
You still lay here with me beneath the willow tree
I am the sun-bleached leaves and gnarled bark
Your hands—long and thin, the willow's branches—entangle mine
Fingertips icy from immersing beneath
My hands, rough, warm yours
Your chuckle makes me squeeze tighter
Pulling me ever-deeper into your leaves

Zahra Linsky

An east wind whispers through blades of grass
You are the willow's howling, rustling, singing leaves
Curls of your hair cloud your face
But your smile—the root of your being—remains free from shrouding
Like the willow, you belong only to the soil and water
If the breeze blows just right,
Your seeds will spread far and wide
For now, you are the sturdy trunk, kept immobile but fed by stories
    from across the land

The willow tree caresses us as the sun dips deeper
And the river runs cool
As reedy boats float past, you wrap your branches around me
We sink into willow roots

bigfoot hunting

Early morning sun gleaned the fur of a golden retriever through a windshield, welcoming the day in orange light. The dog panted. It was yet another day of travel, but he was more than ready for it after all those hours yesterday in the car. He stretched his back as his owner, Levi, leaned down to grab the skin by his spine.

"Aw, Tucker? Are you tired?" she cooed.

He looked up at her with wild brown eyes. The excitement of another hike was upon them, and they'd make the most of it. He howled in excitement as Levi opened the car door for him to run around in the meadow grass.

Levi dropped to the ground to rub his face. She put a finger to her lips, shushing him. "Be quiet, baby boy. Avalon is still asleep," she whispered.

Tucker jumped as an arm slammed out of the Jeep window. From the backseat, Avalon groaned. Her voice was crackly from a night of restless sleep. "You guys are such morning people! It's the crack of dawn. No one should be up and moving yet."

"It may be morning, but we've gotta get into the woods soon," Levi said. She patted down her pockets before pulling out a map. It crinkled as she opened it. "It's now or never."

Avalon slumped against the car's window frame. "One week of spring break left."

"Our last one."

"I can't believe senior year is almost over. High school's passed us by in a—" Avalon snapped her fingers.

When they first met in seventh grade, Avalon smiled the widest she could, braces and all. Her shirt was covered with various cryptids, though some of the design began to wear off several months prior. She approached Levi with an outstretched hand.

"I heard your name was Leviathan," Avalon said. "I wanna hunt Bigfoot. Will you come with me?"

That day, the girls made a pact. They wouldn't come to fulfill it until they both neared eighteen.

#

With packs on their shoulders and Tucker's leash wrapped around the straps, Levi and Avalon stepped between uneven patches of grass. It'd be a few miles before they reached the foot of the mountain.

"You're sure he's been sighted around here?" Avalon asked. With the sun bright on her forehead, she sweated.

Levi crinkled the map between her fingers. It was her only lifeline out here, as there was little cellular connection if any. "I wouldn't bring us a full day away from home if I wasn't certain. All the sites I use show signs of him sighted here."

"Someone could just be baiting you to come and kidnap us."

"They don't even know I'm a girl. We all just want to find Bigfoot— if it's the next guy or me, it still helps to share information."

Tucker whined a quarter of a mile ahead of them. His head was low, a sign of fear. Levi smiled. He hated being without her—one of her favorite things about him. He'd have to wait, though. The sun announced it was time for Shacharit—morning—prayers.

Levi stopped to pull out her siddur. She may not have any connection to society, but for the time being, she could focus on connecting to the world around her. Avalon listened along as Levi chanted her blessings, joking around when she asked Levi to finish them with a request to HaShem to help them find Bigfoot.

"Bigfoot is my problem. Not HaShem's."

Avalon laid back on the grass. Wildflowers tickled her neck. "You should at least give tzedakah now before we're free from data completely." She tossed a crumpled piece of paper at Levi.

The prayer on it read:

> Rabbi Binyamin said: All are presumed blind until the Holy One, blessed be He, enlightens their eyes. We know this from the verse: "G-d opened her eyes and she went and filled up the water skin."
>
> G-d of Meir answer me! x3
>
> In the merit of the charity which I am donating for the sake of the soul of Rabbi Meir the Miracle Worker may I find Bigfoot which I have lost.

Levi's rabbi thought this would be the best prayer to recite before they continued their journey, though he had some issues about how it applied to finding a cryptid.

She caught a phone as Avalon tossed it to her. It was open to a website, prefilled with a donation of $18. She clicked donate, and then it was complete.

"Hopefully, this is enough. I've been reading psalm one-hundred-and-twenty-one daily for thirty-nine days now."

Levi lent Avalon her hand to stand up. The both of them held eye contact; this could be their only attempt at their childish dream.

#

The forest deepened around them as Tucker weaved between their legs. Levi careened her head toward the sky, watching for the birds flitting between the trees. They were especially active, which no one on the forums had mentioned. Were birds a sign of Bigfoot?

Nah, that couldn't be it. Avalon would laugh at her if she said that aloud.

Still, she fidgeted with the notebook in her back pocket. Other hunters could find it helpful in case they were successful today.

"What if we find a bear?" Avalon said. "A lot of people think they've found Bigfoot, but in reality, they just found a bear."

"Then we hope it doesn't see us and then keep on going."

Bigfoot was out there. That much Levi felt in her heart. Though, hearts couldn't be trusted. They were fickle and weak to whims and impulses.

Levi glanced at Avalon.

At least the tongue could be trusted not to be so outward about Levi's emotions. Instead, it let her say, "Do you remember when we first made plans for this in sophomore year?"

Avalon shifted the weight of her backpack. "It's been a while, but yeah. I remember you having your head on my lap."

Levi remembered that night all too well. Her tongue had almost failed her, but Avalon remained unaware of what bubbled in her heart. At least, that's what Levi guessed.

"We made so many lists. I found my favorite forums, and you created wish lists for us to buy all our supplies. We wouldn't have been able to get this far if it weren't for you."

Avalon elbowed her. "You're the one with a license."

A body of silky fur slipped between Avalon's legs. Tucker whined until Avalon ducked down to rub his chin and teeth. She added, "And you brought your baby."

Tucker's too-small ears tucked back—his smile.

Their final location was a day away, so Levi looked for places to camp overnight as they hiked. Most of this area would be too dark at night for Tucker to make his way around. His eyesight was ordinarily good, but the vet said Levi had to be careful with him at night. So she carried him as the forest deepened and darkened.

She and Avalon traded him off until the forest finally let them back into a meadow. This one stretched across a valley within this mountain range. A twinkle of sunlight reflected against the far-away lake. Levi guessed that they'd have to cross over the outpouring river at a few points, but that could be managed with Tucker on her hip and her shoes tied to her backpack.

The green of the valley welcomed them with open arms.

#

When the final flash of daylight dipped below the horizon, Levi stretched her arms toward the sky. She tried to act calm so Avalon and Tucker would be, but she worried.

They still hadn't set up camp. Soon, they'd have to use flashlights. If Bigfoot were around, he'd be scared away.

So they wandered. Levi broke out her father's flashlight—the $50 one he used at work—and Avalon kept close by, Tucker in her arms. He nuzzled his nose into her neck. The chill of night, though upon them, couldn't affect him through his thick coat.

Crunch.

Avalon jumped. "Did you hear that?" she squeaked.

Levi crouched as she whispered, "That wasn't Bigfoot."

It couldn't be. The reports of him in this area never mentioned this kind of crunching—a noise so deep, sounding like a log breaking in half through weight alone. Nothing on the forums said anything about this.

Then who was it?

A deer? A bear? A person?

The last one scared Levi more than anything. She tugged on Avalon's sweater toward the sound of rushing water. If they crossed, then whoever was nearby wouldn't be able to follow their tracks. Hopefully. Levi switched off her flashlight.

Low to the ground, they kept an eye out for whatever could have made that noise. But shelter would be a priority still. Without the flashlight, they'd be useless for most of the night, especially once nightfall truly began.

Levi urged Avalon to run ahead as she watched around. The forums, the reports, the documentaries—nothing prepared her for this. She was at her weakest so far from society.

"Levi!" Avalon hissed. "Get over here. I found shelter."

Avalon and Tucker waited tucked between two trees with moonlight illuminating their faces. The glow of light led Levi's eyes to the glimpse of a window.

A cabin in the woods. The shelter horror used to scare people. If the source of the noise was a person, this could be their home. But, more likely than not, it was just some forest animal trying to survive. They must not like it when two girls infringed upon their home, damaging the local flora.

Levi chanted this to herself as she crept toward the house. She was unarmed, which probably wasn't a good idea if that sound turned out to be from a person.

She hesitated before opening the door. The handle shook in her hands.

It opened to an open-layout home, empty if not for a mattress overgrown with mold. Levi flicked on her flashlight and checked every corner. It seemed safe enough for Avalon and Tucker to come inside. After that, she could scout the outside.

"It's fine. Dirty, but I think it's safe," Levi said as she pushed open the door. Her flashlight was off so they wouldn't be blinded as they walked inside. "Carry Tucker inside. There might be glass."

Avalon nodded. She scooped Tucker a little higher on her chest, pressing his forehead into her neck. From this distance, Levi couldn't hear what she whispered to him, but she assumed it would be loving.

As Levi pushed the door back, the handle dug into the base of her spine. That would ache some tomorrow.

Once those two were inside, she pressed her flashlight against her chest. One, two, three deep breaths before she could manage to step past the wall and look around. The moonlight shone brighter here.

Both the clearing at the front of the cabin and the wooded area in the back were free from any markings larger than a hoof. Humans hadn't been here in years. That was comforting—but also a bit nerve-wracking—to Levi.

Why did no one live in this cabin—not even squatters? Was there a murder? Was this area prone to earthquakes?

No, this area hasn't had a significant earthquake in over a hundred years. These mountains were formed too slowly for that.

Levi brushed her face clear of her brown hair, though it just stuck onto her neck instead.

Tonight, they just needed shelter—a safe one. Cleanliness could be subjective in these woods.

#

Morning filtered in with the dawn through cracked windows. The lines stretched across Avalon's cheek. Her breaths were slow and soft within her sleeping bag—a restful night after a long day.

Levi watched her with a small smile. Her hand strayed at the edge of her sleeping bag, waiting to reach over and touch that soft blonde hair of hers. But that'd probably wake Avalon up, and for now, Levi wanted to avoid that. The day ahead would be just as tiring, but in the evening, they'd finally make it to the lake.

Bigfoot was within their grasp.

Six years of waiting was within their grasp.

She could almost taste it. Those sleepless nights of research brought them to this moment—to this morning—to this marvel.

When Levi first started planning this with Avalon, neither had complete faith that it would happen. They both thought of it in middle school as a fantasy they'd love to try but never achieve, like a month-long trip to Europe.

Avalon was the first to propose that they get it done. The very first forum the two of them scoured was one Avalon found, though it turned out to be a bust. Too many people wanted to advertise for their cheaply-made Bigfoot documentaries and all the clickbait that came with it. Too few truly cared about finding him.

When Levi shuffled through her backpack for her siddur, she carefully set each item down with the greatest caution. Waking up Avalon and Tucker felt like a sin, even if it wasn't one. Besides, her heart raced as she imagined finally being able to search for Bigfoot.

The chill of the mountains greeted her cheeks, warming them to a rosy pink. With the evening fog fading as the sun rose ever-higher, the blessings of the day were finally upon her.

Facing the rising sun, Levi thanked HaShem for these blessings in a solo Shacharit service. Her excitement grew sweeter in her mouth when she bowed at the end of the Amidah.

A day of warmth was ahead of her. A day of searching and a day of walking through trails lost to time, overgrown with young seedlings.

Levi became aware of Avalon once she finished Shacharit. Her friend was sitting on the grass a few meters behind her, basking in the

sunlight. The colors of the world became all the richer when they shone on Avalon.

She kneeled where she had stood. "Hey, when'd you wake up?"

"Not long ago," Avalon said. She stared at the pink-purple clouds, braiding her hair absentmindedly. "It was nice to hear you pray. You're so calming."

Levi's chin rested on her fist as she watched Avalon. "I can't believe you're so sweet. All these years, and I would've thought you'd get tired of me at some point."

"Oh, Leviathan." Avalon leaned forward, pressing on her soft thighs. Her sun-kissed cheeks grew pink with blush and a smile. "I could never get tired of you."

#

After a quick breakfast, they circled the cabin in increasing diameters to search for any sign of the sound last night, or better yet, Bigfoot. It's been weeks since those forum posts agreed that he was in this area, so it could be possible for him to make it from the lake down to this part of the valley. Well, that was if this area had the food he survived on. No one knew what Bigfoot ate—just that, to sustain his body, he had to eat thousands of calories a day.

Avalon, Tucker, and Levi packed up the cabin by the time the sun was directly overhead. It'd be time for Mincha soon, but that could come when they were closer to the lake. The sun wouldn't set until almost eight tonight. By then, they would have set up their camp and watched the slight laps of lake water against the shore.

"You know, I wish we found him today. That was a few hours of walking in circles, yet nothing," Levi said.

The path they took through the forest was rockier than before, and too many fallen trees marred their way.

"Maybe he's found a nice cave up near the lake. He'd have no reason to come down here, where the habitat could potentially be less habitable," Avalon suggested.

"Still."

"Still?" She cocked her head as she glanced at Levi, almost hitting a branch because of her shift of focus. "Jesus."

"HaShem yishmor," Levi whispered. "I know I shouldn't feel this way because I'm still having fun with you, but this trip itself is just me getting my hopes up before they inevitably fall." She tapped her fingers against her backpack straps. Everything felt so tight.

Avalon elbowed her. "Look up ahead."

As Levi lifted her head, Tucker bolted into the bushes. He was after something, but that something wasn't human. That much she knew from his reaction.

Bigfoot?

She pressed against a nearby tree, fishing her phone out of her pocket. If this were him, then she wouldn't miss one moment of it. She lifted it over her eyes before swinging around to follow Tucker's trail.

He ran toward the nearby river. Levi skidded to slow down on loose gravel.

Glances showed that his barks weren't toward anything six to eight feet tall. Not even to something five feet tall.

It was a deer. Only four feet at most.

Its wide black eyes met Levi's brown ones before it sprinted through the river. The deer fell for a brief moment. Past the camera, she reached for it.

Tucker's ears perked up when Avalon reached the top of the riverbank. She panted as he barked in excitement. Strands of hair fell out of her ponytail. Dirty, but still beautiful. I averted my eyes to refocus on the deer.

Avalon pointed at the deer with shaky fingers. "We should follow it. Horses always know the best path to cross rivers—why shouldn't deer?"

"But it stumbled."

"Do you think you know better than a resident of the forest?" Avalon pointed out.

Levi pursed her lips. "No…"

"Then let's just follow it. We might be able to get to the lake faster, that way." Avalon offered Levi her hand. Her skin was soft and squishy, reminding Levi of all those nights they spent curled up in her twin-size bed.

There were only a few months of those nights left.

#

Their hike led them deeper into the forest, up a great mountain that left all three of them panting. Tucker's ears tucked back as he ran back and forth between Avalon, Levi, and the trail ahead. Sunlight dappled his fur between trees. Avalon chased him through thick bushes, her cheeks rosy-pink with laughter. She scooped him up as they crossed a stream and arrived at a flatter slope.

Levi hung back with her hands in her pockets as she watched Avalon and Tucker play in the grass. Together, they were like child and puppy again. Avalon held Tucker high above her head before setting him down to look at the ground. Levi followed, her smile slowly building as she drew closer.

Avalon crouched at a collection of lilac. Petals flattened between her fingers. "Do you remember these?"

"You got them for my seventeenth birthday." Levi picked one off its stem and put it behind Avalon's ear. Its lilac complimented the gold sheen of her hair. "They're always going to remind me of you."

The lilac shifted as Avalon titled her head to look at Levi. She smiled wide. "That's why I got them for you."

"To think we'd find it out in the wild like this—it's almost meant to be, isn't it?"

Tucker, irritated by the lack of attention, pushed between them. He whined until Levi put a flower in his collar and called him a good boy.

"I'm delighted you adopted him," Avalon said. She rubbed his chin, barely touching his teeth.

Following the cool breeze that blew through the mountain range, Levi reminisced about when she first brought Tucker home. Avalon had been the first one to suggest that they take him on hikes. "He could be a good buddy for Bigfoot hunting," she had said in jest. Back then, back in freshman year, they had no idea if they would ever set out on a private expedition.

But here they were, with windswept hair and skin warmed by the noonday sun. Levi tucked a bud of lilac in the side pocket of her pack. When they got home, she'd press it and hang it up on the wall. Maybe she'd bring it with her to college… It was hard to believe that, next fall, she'd be without Avalon and Tucker at her side.

"Leviathan," Avalon called. She had taken down her hair, letting it flutter in the wind. She matched Tucker, whose tail wagged back and forth as the breeze slowed and sped up. "You're too slow. Come on!"

"Coming!" I yelled back.

Even if we couldn't spend all year together, side by side, they still had this moment together. Time couldn't take that away from her.

#

When the lake finally bloomed ahead of them, Levi let out a sigh of relief. Some part of her had worried they wouldn't get there before dark, even though there were still hours until sundown.

She wiped sweat from her forehead. There was still the tent and the fire to set up. Though they'd have to be careful, as some forum members said, Bigfoot was afraid of fire. He was like a caveman—utterly unfamiliar to the miracle of the taming of fire.

Levi collected tinder, kindling, logs, and rocks while Avalon set up the tent. Tonight there was no sturdy cabin to protect them from the elements, and whatever lurked in the woods. The breeze came from the east—blowing directly over the chilly lake.

They shivered until it was finally time to curl up in their sleeping bags, Tucker between them. He acted as a living radiator as the wind howled.

"Whether or not we find Bigfoot, I'm okay with it," Avalon said.

Levi opened one eye. The weight of sleep was upon her, but she wanted to hear what Avalon had to say. "What do you mean?"

"I know we've wanted to find him ever since seventh grade, but this still means something, right? Like that's six years of a journey. Six years of searching. All the time, I was with you." Her hand reached over the edge of the sleeping bag—doing something Levi didn't have the guts to do earlier. "I'm okay if he doesn't turn out to be real because you're real."

Her hand reached across Tucker, resting along the edge of Levi's sleeping bag. This was the moment. She grasped Avalon's hand. "I'm so glad I met you."

\#

The following morning came with a chill and fog, but that made all three more excited to start their day. They'd spend this time would be spent together.

The search for Bigfoot began.

rocky garden

arisen from the earth is a garden of sticks and skeletons
their phalanges intertwined with roses
horizon to horizon, the skeletons waltz between rocks, through stone
    rivers
my fleshless prince dresses me in a moss-grown
her arms tap against mine as she decorates my hair with spider lilies
woven into intricate knots
skeleton men play flutes with empty exhales
to sing the celebration of espousal postmortem
and together, we venture to an entrance grave
the grassy hill above us sighs with shaking roots
growing, burgeoning deeper into our home
my prince crowns me with stems of minerals
falling into an endless rest within an endless garden
tending to our bones

godskin

Every night, bioluminescent waves crash onto the sand, and every night Enbar waits for Ransmal to arrive. She sits in the crook of driftwood tonight, hair strewn by the wind. This will be her last chance.

—that's what had Ransmal said last time. She had picked up his pieces and held them together like glass and broken pottery. Each crack shone gold against his glowing cerulean skin. Imperfect. But the Divine were supposed to be perfect. Another crack in his skin, another crack in her trust.

She sees him against the moon at first tonight: a series of rotating rings engraved with symbols. His flaming core burns her eyes as he melts into something human-like. Mankind's perception of him changes with the phases of the moon; no one person sees him the same way. He likes that. And he likes that Enbar doesn't mind that no one else knows about him. He is her secret.

water shone around him, absorbing every bit of who he was: angelic, godly. what feeble minds could only dream of.

"The sea parts as he steps foot onto land"—though, that is a misconception. Ransmal had laughed when she told him this, shortly after

47

they first met. That's only what her eyes perceived, not the actuality. He never touches mortality; he is far above them all.

Prophet, Ransmal calls her. He presses a nail below her eye, welling up crimson blood. Beneath him, beneath all he knew. And yet, he found himself returning night after night to meet this Prophet of his.

"Evening," he says. He doesn't know the word 'hello.'

Enbar curls her knees into her chest. "Do you ever forget what it's like?"

Gods don't have eyes, but she knows he watches her. He leans back on one hand, the knee opposite propped up. "I've never been as happy as when I bleed. It reminds me of you."

"That isn't what I'm asking."

"Yes, but that's what you mean." She can't predict his patterns, what he'll say next. His existence is as confusing as eclipses. Ransmal once claimed that the Divine couldn't be understood by mortality, but Enbar is starting to think that he just didn't want to explain himself. "I was never like you, Lovely. You're—" He glances at her body, the freckles and scars. The only proof she has that he is alive was the spiraling gold on her clavicle. Glimmers of gold in her irises. His blood purifies her. No longer can he blind her.

> temples and cathedrals and worshipping ants. hoops he
> passed through were only a moment in his existence.
> immortality was a sin.

"Why are you abandoning me, then?"

"I have to." He presses his scalding hand against her cheek. Any more pressure and the water inside her will boil, yet she is safe. "There are things I'm not allowed to tell you, and by all gods above, I know they'd kill me if I tried. I wouldn't be able to see you again that way."

"I hope your plans have changed. It wouldn't feel nice to know you wanted to hurt me all along." She presses her hand against his; he is sunburnt skin in summer. "You're going to leave. I was only a plaything—your promises are empty."

"I—I have to."

"Or, I could join you. You don't need to alone up…" The sky rumbles. "There."

they said his domain was the sky and the sea and jelly-fish and soaring condors. the land was for impurity and his sister-gods, hiding inside trees and waiting for the right person to pull beneath the moss.

Seven seconds pass before lightning strikes the far-off ocean.

"I could go with you, Ransmal. You promised me I could be with you. Be like you."

"—That's what I said to get you to be quiet. I was born like this, I think. And you're a prophet. What I told you and what you want to believe will influence generations." He shakes her shoulders. "You could lie, and everyone would think you're crazy or blessed, but they'll follow you all the same. Being a messenger for the gods is a rare opportunity."

"I'll make sure you find a home out there. One where you can start your own religion."

Enbar shrugs off his comment like a rock brushes off a wave. Her eyes harden.

"So everyone could worship you like the one true god? I won't stroke your ego. I know what I am to you."

"Dear, do you think I haven't considered this? I can't sleep like you, so all these quiet nights, I've been wondering what this means." He tugs at his hair, though perhaps it wasn't hair. His appearance constantly shifts; this form—this human shape—was what he thought she'd trust him the most with. Other Prophets preferred amorphous beings. When

49

they met, all she wanted was a friend. "Besides, you have a family to get back to. They want to know who you're sneaking off every night for. They'd kill you if they knew it was me."

She rolls her eyes, waving her hand at distant pools.

"People will kill me either way. I'll become a martyr in your name, and decades later, people will find my crazed ramblings inspiring and found your religion." Her face freezes—a glimmer of an idea in her eyes.

"I'll be a god, like you."

> sister-gods slipped him a liquor so sweet it may as well
> been godblood. he sipped into a realm of lost memories
> and brine—they coat his skin with kisses and warmth
> until all he thinks of is sparks

Ransmal shifts onto his far arm. Being too close to humans was a reason for consequence. "I don't know if humans can become gods. I don't… I'm fairly sure that wasn't how I was created."

"But how do you know? There are dryads in the trees and nymphs of the seas. They're within your domain. You made them. You could do the same for me."

"Enbar, I don't think you understand. I'm a new god. I may be as old as you, relatively speaking, but no human has ever been among the heavens. They wouldn't survive there," he says.

The heavens were too hot for any human to handle. They'd burn and burn and burn until all that was left was the sliver of their soul, but even then, they'd be crushed by the pressure. The gates of the afterlife turned those souls away.

"Then the gods have never tried. No way to prove your statement true." Enbar puts her ring-clad hand on his thigh. Her cold stare of determination outweighs the sting.

Ransmal looks at the moon. "I don't want to take that chance. I care about you, I promise—"

"Your promises mean nothing to me. If you cared, then you would be sitting on the driftwood next to me."

He twists his ring around his finger but then sits down next to her. So close that the heat almost burns. "I'm doing this because I don't want to see you dead by immortal hands. The dryads whisper, Enbar. They swear not to tell, but if another god confronted them, our secrets would be laid bare. I'll be here, even if you can't see me. Please trust me in this."

"You ask me that like you'd even give me a choice." Ever since they first met, his words were sweet with coercion. She fell into his riptide before she even noticed, too in love with those glowing hands to swim to shore. "If I had known this was your plan all along, I would've stopped trying so hard."

to become a god is to dress in the flesh of the another—
to contain glow and dreams and the ever-changing sea
within a body so small and tight. to whisper stories into
mortals' ears, twist perceptions, lose what you thought
you had gained.

Hovering above her, he presses his hand against her cheek. "Have I ever told you anything but the truth? You'll achieve all you desire. That's why I blessed you. Among all men, it is you who looks at me without fear. Every second you're with me, the Divine are satiated."

Enbar glances away. "That may be your will, but it's not mine. I've been waiting to learn something tangible from you. Something that would stop mortals from resenting the Divine. Why wouldn't humans hate something they don't understand?" She knew almost as little as them.

"They blame me for their follies and insult me in their prayers. I can't save every human," he says. "I've tried explaining."

She scoffs. "That's the first time I've heard you refer to the Divine as yourself alone."

"The Divine—we chose you because you're beyond anything we've ever seen." He reaches toward her.

"How do I make them believe if I can't?"

"We have more to say, but all good things come in due time. The tides haven't been in your favor," he says.

"Really?" she says. "You're a god; you control the tides. You're everything I dream of and more. I told myself being blind to your plans was a good thing, but every choice you made for me caused my family to avoid me more."

Ransmal takes off his ring and holds it out to her. Like his Divine form, it hovers above his palm. "Prophets read the signs. Prophets understand the favors the Divine have promised them."

"Your words don't mean anything. I believed in you. I trusted you. But you cheated me the first time you lied about the people I grew up with." Enbar thumbs her ring; he'd given it to her during their first meeting. She regrets ever putting it on. "When we first met, you told me I had promise. You promised me I would be great. But I know now that gods lie as much as men."

"You—" Ransmal reaches for her arm, but she tears it away. "You could've had everything."

She laughs, her voice hoarse. "You made me realize gods aren't worth believing in. Find yourself a new Prophet. Maybe she'll actually believe your bullshit."

Enbar slips her ring off. It glimmers as golden as her eyes until she throws it to the sand at his feet. "I'm done."

"The Divine will be waiting for your return, Prophet." Ransmal presses her ring into his palm.

"If you want me back, prove it." She leaves the beach on a night as dark as their first meeting.

#

Later, she finds a silent home and her ring coated in Divine ichor.

ruins

down the old wisteria lane
where butterflies bloomed like delicate blossoms
she said through teeth
to welcome pink water when it arrives
to use it
and to pour it down the drain

I should have realized it before
she took my hand
led me to cliffs where patches of daises
grew between our toes
but her palm was so warm
she wrapped her hands around me
like mother holds child
and pushed
kicked us off the cliff's edge
squeezed me tighter
tears wet my shoulder
nails tore into my spine

Zahra Linsky

we fell like flowers
our petals spinning in dizzying arrays

her blood ran pink across my fingers
a near match of the sky at sunset

I once wondered what death was like
but here she was, in my arms
pouring herself until her shell wilted
a corpse violet and white
among the copse of wisteria lane

nothing but a king and her ruins

54

that which spreads

A boy sat surrounded by deer, the snow brown and rusty pink beneath their feet. Two elk horns curled out of his head and weighed down his frail neck. A woolen pullover collar brushed against his cheeks, and when he breathed, hot air puffed into the surrounding air.

That's what I saw as I hopped the fence onto the Treus House property. Out here, the forest grew so dense that snow hardly reached the forest floor. But Treus House stood apart—not a single tree grew within ten meters of it from all directions. That's why we Baardians set up a fence around it.

Well, that and the other reason.

I brushed off my trousers and straightened my spine. The trail I followed—the one worn thinner with each passing spring—led directly to the Boy. He watched me through long eyelashes.

"You visit me yet again, though you forget the consequences?" he said. He brushed his hair out of his face to reveal patches of soil and freckles.

I stuck my hands in my pockets, fiddling with a loose thread. "What can I say? I got dared again."

As he spoke, a fawn set its head into his lap. "You really are so feeble-minded."

"And? My friends are watching me. I'll go into the cursed house and talk to the creepy man who lives there. I'm not a chicken."

He cracked a smile on his cracked lips. "The deer are hungry this time of year, but go ahead. The house stands empty."

"Hmpf." My fingers tightened across my satchel strap, digging my fingernails into my rough palms. This time, the dare included bringing something back, even though I wouldn't remember taking it. Be that what it may—cowardice wasn't something I wanted to take home with me, either.

The steps up to the House creaked, just as I always thought they would. When I watched my friends try to reach the Treus House, this was the furthest they got. They hesitated on the rotting wood before running back with their tails between their legs, their ears covered with puckered fingers. Only fools went inside. And only fools talked to the Horned Boy.

At the end of the creaky porch, there stood a door. It opened as soon as I rested a fingertip on the handle. None of the boys had come this far before. I squeezed my eyes shut as I pushed it open.

The house was barren, as most of us had suspected. Out of Jurryt, Achim, and I, Achim had the role of the daydreamer of the House's innards. He thought there'd be bones and pipe smoke and crumbling portraits. Telling him about this would be a disappointment. The walls had no decoration unless water damage counted as decor. I brushed my hand across the thin table pressed against a wall. Like I guessed, my fingertips were coated with dust. Did the Boy even live inside here?

This room looked to be a dining and living area unlike those in my village. We normally had tables and appropriate seating in the center of the room, but all the furniture here was pressed against the wall. Scuff marks marred the floorboards. Exactly as Mama always told me. She raised me on tales of the Treus House and now had the gall to expect me to not want to visit.

Crouching down, I traced the marks. They ran as deep as my second knuckle. A primordial fear cracked in my chest.

I scrambled up tilted steps to the second story. Unlike the first one, leaves and bark littered the hall. There were at least four rooms up here, but each door was closed. Being in a room with the Boy's deer, in case they slept there, could only be a last resort. I took a large piece of bark and scuttled out.

The Boy watched me as I left. This time, the deer who surrounded him stood up. "Be careful. Take from the deer and they'll be able to find you again."

I brushed off his warning. I wouldn't remember it by the evening, anyway.

My friends rushed to greet me as soon as I crossed the fence. Achim took my satchel from my shaking hands. "Minke! He didn't do anything to you, did he?"

Jurryt wrapped my arm around his shoulders. Now that he lifted the burden of my weight, I felt my knees break out of their locked position. "We saw you talking with him. Please tell us if he said anything weird to you—before you forget."

I swiped my hand against my forehead and tried to focus my vision on the snow ahead of me. Step by step.

These boys were right to be concerned. By nightfall, anyone who had stepped foot onto the Treus House property would forget all that had happened there. By nightfall, every threat he told me had to be remembered by others, or else I'll face the consequences. By nightfall, the deer could make their move.

#

I kept my head down when I got home. By the dust all over my legs and on my boots, my parents were sure to know where I'd been.

My room lay on the far edge of the house. This building was like the Treus House in that its structure was unusual for the area. Unlike the Treus House, it was unlike Baarda homes in that we had more than one door leading out. Luckily, I had direct access to my room from the outdoors.

More time to brace for impact.

Mama was sitting on my bed when I stepped inside. Like usual, her auburn hair was braided back, and her lips pressed tight into a grimace. "You said you'd stop going back there."

I put my hands up in defense. "My friends…"

"Young lady, you're too old to keep on blaming your friends for something you wanted to do. If they're so bad and keep coercing you, then you would've broken up with them by now." Mama narrowed her all-encompassing gaze. For this moment, I knew there was nothing but me and the Treus House on her mind.

I shrugged off my coat in an effort to ease the stale tension, hanging it on the back of a chair. "I keep telling you, Mama, that house isn't even that dangerous. I went insi—"

Between blinks, she had gotten up from my bed to hold me by my collar. "You went inside?"

One by one, I pried her fingers off. "Yes. As I was saying, I went inside and I'm totally fine. The house wasn't even that unusual. Just dusty."

Mama lifted my arms and checked under my collar as if shaking out any secrets I wore. "No scratches… Is that all you did there?"

I squeezed my eyes shut as I spoke. "No. The boys dared me to talk to the Horned Boy."

"Minke! You know what he'll do to you," she said.

"He didn't threaten me if that's what you're insinuating." I was careful to hold my tongue for anything past a quick summary of events. Even saying "or anything" would be a lie. The Boy warned me. "We're hours from sunset, so I remember everything clearly enough."

She sat back down and sighed. "Why do you have to keep on doing all these dangerous things? If you don't get hurt this time, that doesn't mean you won't get hurt next time."

I knew that. Mama knew I did. But couldn't listen. "I'm starting to think all the stories about the Treus House are nothing more than rumors and old wives tales."

"It's not just gossip. Have I ever told you about the Laninga's eldest son?"

I sat on my bed beside her, sinking into the soft blankets. "No. I thought they only had daughters." All were around my parents' age by now, one even the mother of Jurryt.

Mama tapped her thumbs against each other. One, two, three

58

breaths before she spoke. "He was the firstborn and one of your father's closest friends. As all dumb kids do, they dared each other to go up to the Treus House's front door.

"The Laninga's son went first. He only made it up to the first step before the Horned Boy and his deer bit into his calves and spine." She balled her fists. "Your father ran away, rightfully so. But every few days, he came back to see if the body was still there. Bit by bit, bone by bone, those deer ate that poor boy whole."

Her body shook. It took my mind a moment to catch up with what my eyes saw. Mama was crying.

"I was going to marry that dumb boy, you know," she cracked out. "Ever since we were kids, I had my heart set on him. He promised me we'd marry as adults. But what is love for? He went and got himself killed instead."

"Mama..."

She wiped her eyes, straightened her back. "I'm sorry. This isn't the kind of story kids should hear about."

"I'm almost an adult," I corrected.

"I wouldn't have done my job as your mother if you became all grown up yet still acted like this."

There wasn't anything I could say to argue with her. She was right. I took too many chances. People talked about those who lost their bets.

My mother, a tall yet slender woman. Her cheeks wrinkled at the corners of her lips. All the clothing she wore—everything I wore, too— was made by her hands. I couldn't bring the town upon her like that.

Her cracked lips started moving before I realized she caught me staring at her. I put my head down. "Is there something you wanted to ask me?"

"Has the Horned Boy ever aged?"

Mama tapped her chin. "He's always been a boy, I think. Ever since he first arrived."

Arrived? "When was that?"

"Sweetie, I don't know. As far as I'm aware, he's always been around. My grandma told me the same stories about him that her grandmother told her."

"Could you tell me those stories again, sometime?" My voice was low, hesitant.

She stood up and offered me her hand. "Sure, sometime. Now come help me with dinner. We're having a big meal, and I could use your help."

#

Nikolas, my younger brother, wouldn't take his eyes off me at dinner that night. "Have you forgotten yet?"

"You asked me a moment ago." I pointed my fork at him. "You think I wouldn't realize it if I forgot?"

He pointed his fork right back at me. "First off, I asked, 'Do you remember?' last time. Secondly, you didn't realize that you forgot before. Knowing you, you're bound to do that again."

"A kid shouldn't be talking down to me like that."

"Yeah, and? You aren't an adult yet." He scoffed. "Kids these days turn sixteen and think they're practically grown up."

"You're *twelve.*"

"Who cares? Besides, the sun is soon to set." Outside our kitchen window, a haze bread across snowy hills. The night will be pitch-black, the thick clouds tell me.

"Who have you told about what happened there?" Nik asked.

The sun's rays scattered across trees and quiet homes. The house closest to us had all but one room in the dark. But the lit room had no people inside.

"Minke? Are you awake?"

Out of the corner of my eye, I watched Mama put her hand on Nik's shoulder. "Her friends and me, honey."

"Can you tell me?" he said.

She retracted her hand. "No." Fiddling with the handle of a spoon, she added, "Your father's late tonight."

Nik shrugged. "Sometimes, hunters have to stay out all night to catch their prey. Meat's hard to find during winter."

"His food is getting cold." This meal was for him, I could tell. Mama wanted Father relaxed when she told him what I've done. "He'll be back soon enough."

The rays flickered like a candle as the fog, no longer weakened by daytime warmth, grew thicker. Our neighbors melted into the ever-growing mass of evergreen trees. On a night like this, there wouldn't be a moon, even if we could see one.

"Night has fallen," I said.

Nik pointed his fork at me again, ignoring Mama's sigh. "Do you remember?"

I glanced back through the window. A couple of stars watched me back. "I do."

The Horned Boy's threat—his warning—lingered fresh in my mind. His deer can track me now. I fingered the bark in my trouser pocket. Jurryt must have slipped it in before we separated.

"What did you do today?" he clarified.

"I went inside the Treus House and talked to the Boy who lives there."

Mama and Nik exchanged glances. All of us had a single thought: How did Minke remember?

I set the bark on the table. "Mama, did any of the stories your grandma told you mention anything about someone remembering?"

"Not one."

#

Dawn came and went. In my nightgown, I checked on the other rooms, just in case the deer had broken in overnight. Nik slept on the floor in our living space after a rough night. Mama was alone in her bedroom, no husband to warm her and keep her company. Her blanket felt thin in my hands as I tugged it over her. Normally, Father would be the one to do that. But, as a hunter, he had more important things to do.

Snow piled inches away from the front door. I stepped into it hesitantly, freezing my bare souls as I stepped deeper int o the snow. Nik and the boys will have fun playing in this today.

The nighttime fog had mostly cleared by now, but it remained heavy by the treeline. There was movement there, but forests were always full of movement, even during the winter.

I knelt, the cold of snow quickly soaking through my only layer. At this time of day, when light shone blue rather than yellow, hardly any-

one left their homes. It was winter, after all. Not everyone had work to be done. I shifted onto the balls of my feet when I noticed a path across the snow, about a dozen feet in front of me.

It led away from the rest of the village, whose homes stretched toward the peak of the large hill on which we lived. Down here, where the slope eased into a shallow incline, farmers and hunters lived. Few farmers attempted work during this season and the hunters hadn't returned, so whose footsteps were those?

I shivered as I trudged through fresh, pristine snow. My feet ached from sitting outside, but there was a certain unease coming from those steps marring the landscape.

Each step remained thin as I grew closer. With humans, you'd be able to see huge indents for a single step. These were gentler. Almost graceful. I peered inside. Hoofprints.

Where were the deer?

A heavy *plop* of snow slid off an evergreen. The other houses' smoke barely puffed through the frigid air. It froze my throat as my eyes wandered. Rocks, stocky weeds, a lone bug, the chitter of birds waiting for spring. Another day, they would have been normal.

Normal deer didn't come from this far past the treeline during winter. Puffs of hot breath clouded my vision. These tracks were so close to the village... Ice pierced my ribs at the thought of what was at the end of them. I ran alongside them as the trail veered into the woods. My footsteps fostered a trail of messy prints behind me, kicking up snow, but the deer prints I followed remained even and calm.

The forest welcomed me with overgrown roots and fallen logs as I ran deeper into it. It was silly to think someone who grew up in the forests of Baarda wouldn't know how to jump and be nimble. If a deer did it, so could I.

Gripping a log's broken branches, I heaved myself over its mossy side. My hands and feet ached from the bark, but that was nothing a good scare couldn't erase.

For, past the logs, there was a sight both gruesome and arresting. A mess of bodies spread across a divot in the landscape. The snow melted beneath warm blood, creating a crimson slush that coalesced into pud-

63

dles at the deepest point. They'd been here a while, I noticed among all the gore. A few moments longer, and I'd put together enough of their clothing and weaponry to recognize that they were hunters from my village.

Trying to recognize the bodies by their faces would be useless. The deer had eaten to the bone, leaving only a disorder of red tissue and eye whites behind.

#

When I told Mama what happened, I didn't have it in me to cry, even though my father's body was almost certainly one of them. She said the cold had gotten to my head and laid me by the fireplace. It was almost time for people to awake, so I couldn't do anything until then.

I stretched my toes, thankful they weren't an indigo and chartreuse mass. Next time I went outside, I'd slip on shoes first. And maybe a coat. The fire licked the air inches away from where I sat. But that wasn't close enough, wasn't warm enough. Maybe if I just reached a little closer—

"Minke! The chieftain's wife is here to see you," Mama called.

I drew my arm back and tucked it against my chest. The searing flame beckoned my fingers as I looked deeper into the writhing mass.

An older woman came in, carrying a wicker basket of worn fabric. I vaguely recognized her appearance, but I knew by the stories told about her, as well as the stories she was said to tell. Jurryt often groaned of his visits to her home. He was to take over the family business, after all. Knowing the chieftain and his wife came with the job. Mama warned my brother and me of how we were to act around her. The children of hunters were not raised to be wolves. Father didn't like how much she wanted from his catches. He'd have no more catches, going forward.

I shook my head to clear it of the unpleasant thought, but it clung to the back of my mind and wouldn't let go.

"Is anything wrong?" Mrs. Daelmans said. Her green eyes twinkled in the firelight.

"No, ma'am." I hugged my knees closer to my chest. If she took a closer look at my skin, she'd notice day-old scratches. She'd know where I went yesterday and the cause of the hunters' mauling. "Just shaken up."

She knelt beside me. Her delicate hands pulled a blanket from her basket over my shoulders. A cold finger brushed against my neck and I shuddered. "What did you see out there?"

I told her about the tracks and the bodies. Left out the half-eaten eyes and almost bare skulls. Someone would think up scarier details as my story got passed along. By the time I heard it again, it'd be unrecognizable. "There were four, maybe five, bodies. I couldn't tell you who they belonged to." I clutched the blanket tight and drew it over my eyes.

The Horned Boy knew this would happen. All for a stupid piece of bark and I was to blame. Achim and Jurryt might add to the rumor if I was unlucky enough.

Mrs. Daelmans put her hand on my back, rubbing it. "I'll inform the wives of Baarda's hunters by nightfall. Rest up. Moving will only make your bruises hurt more."

My eyes widened as I ducked deeper under the blanket. She saw.

Mama came into the room a few minutes later. "You can't stop her, Minke."

#

The next time I went into the heart of Baarda, my father had not yet returned and children whispered to one another while looking at me. It had been two days since that morning—enough time for me to know my father was one of the dead hunters.

I dressed in the black of mourning as I waded to the chieftain's house. Even with winter and aching feet, this blanket didn't belong to me. So much fine fabric should go back to its owner.

"Minke! Over here!" Jurryt called from my left.

I turned to see him bundled up in a thick scarf and coat, unlike the scrappy clothes he wore when we last visited the Horned Boy. Maybe his mother knew, too.

"Hey, Jurryt." I kept my hands in my pockets as he waved to me. My fingers still ached from climbing over all those logs. The scabs didn't agree with the weather.

He put his hands on my shoulders, eyes wide with a kinder twinkle than Mrs. Daelmans's. "Is it true? Did you find the hunters?"

"About a mile south of my home, yes."

"It was the deer, right?" he said. I nodded. "Do you think the Horned Boy did it?"

"*Shh!* Not so loud. People are suspicious enough of me already." I looked him dead in the eye until he turned away. "What are they saying about me?"

"You seduced a monster to get revenge on your father and, eventually, the whole town." Jurryt tucked his yellowing cap under his arm. All his clothes were hand-me-downs, some appearing as old as the stories my grandmother told my mother. The Horned Boy was older than memory.

"Say, do you know where the Horned Boy came from?" I asked.

He shook his head. "You're asking the wrong person. I'm not one for old wives' tales."

"The Boy is far too tangible to be an old wives' tale."

He waved me off with a grin. Jurryt knew about my father, so his reason for cheerfulness was unknown to me. Though, it would be strange to offer condolences to the cause of her father's murder.

We parted ways as I steeled myself for seeing the chieftain's wife once again. This time, I watched her through an arched window as I drew near. She stood with her back to the panes. Even from her garden gate—the bush-fences slowly withering away—the quality of her clothes remained clear. I clutched the edges of her blanket. No matter how warm and comfortable it was, I couldn't keep it. I could already see Mama being called miserly when she tried to purchase her children cloth.

I knocked on the hawthorn door before I noticed the iron-coated knocker. It had been several years since my last visit, thankfully. I'd narrowly missed several visits due to my poor behavior. Father didn't want people to spread rumors about me. He said I made enough trouble without Mrs. Daelmans knowing.

As she opened the door, I watched the briefest glimpse of her scowl raising into a smile. "Minke! Your mother didn't say you were coming by today."

"I came on my own. Here." I stuck out the hastily folded blanket.

When she had handed it to me, it had been pristine.

Gingerly, Mrs. Daelmans took the blanket from my hands as if picking burrs off her stockings. "Why don't you come in? I've put on a pot of tea."

I shuffled inside. This house seemed to have a fairly open layout on the base floor, like the Treus House. As I followed her to the kitchen, my eyes got caught on painting after painting. Portraits of men and women covered the halls. They dressed in shades of red and orange, all sitting placidly with their eyes shut.

I settled down at a linen-covered table. With my arms folded on the table, I watched Mrs. Daelmans go through the motions of preparing a plate with tea. Staying longer would be a pain, but leaving now would only lead to more rumors. I've heard that, in other towns, rumors were nothing but words. Baarda didn't restrain rumors and stories. I clenched my fists. Our stories felt so much more real.

Mrs. Daelmans sat a teacup in front of me as I drew back my arms. My cheeks burned with the reminder that elbows on the table weren't proper.

"Minke," she said, "why do you keep testing the Horned Boy?"

"I—I do not," I stammered.

She sipped her tea, eyes closed. "Do not think that Baarda doesn't notice. Even with my own ears, I've heard Achim's father scolding him for going up to the Treus House for the thirteenth time. When I asked, the father told me that he watched you closely. He said you're bad news."

She set down her teacup. "Considering what you've done, I'm sure you know there will be consequences."

I stared into the moon of tea. "How do you know what I did? Jurryt and Achim didn't tell anyone."

"I have eyes and ears all across the town, dear."

Without another word, she crossed to the far end of the kitchen. I watched her through the fine wool of her sleeve and the silk of her bodice. Her fine fingers lifted a fatty candlestick off its holder. A flame.

She lit two candles between us. "Without consequences, ask yourself what your mother and brother will be left with." Her mouth opened into a perfect 'O' as she pointed to the ceiling. "Minke, do they know

it's your fault?"

My lip quivered. "No."

"Do they know you talked to the Boy?"

I nodded. Looking her in the eye would be far too painful.

"Do they know you were threatened?" she said with a hint of laughter in her throat.

Mrs. Daelmans's tea burned my tongue. Quickly, I wiped my eyes to hide their watering. "I haven't told them."

"Very well."

She knew that I remembered, or more accurately, never forgot. A way out grew seemingly further and further from my grasp. With shaking legs, I stood, blew out the fire, and grabbed the candlesticks.

If she was going to give me consequences, I could at least finish the Boy off first. That way Mama wouldn't end up with a daughter whose story was all bad.

#

Mama watched me rustle through the pantry, looking for materials we couldn't afford to give up. Oil and fat grew more expensive as the winter drew longer. She folded her arms across her chest. "Minke, do you know what you're doing?"

"Just lock the doors tonight. If you can, shutter the windows closed. If they try hard enough, the deer can break through glass." Jars, no. Boxes, no. The pantry shelves grew messier by the second. My calves strained as I reached for the top shelf.

She handed me the sealed clay jar. I sniffed it, only to find yet another preservative. None of this would do. "Do you know what will happen? Stories don't die."

"There's a wide world out there, Mama. There are more than a few stories that have been lost to memory," I offered.

Mama pulled my shoulders to face our fireplace. On a shelf beside it lay a large jar. I lifted the cork and sniffed. Oil. "Don't tell Nik what I'm doing tonight. I don't want him involved," I said, tucking the jar beneath my arm.

Mama patted my head. "He'll find out sooner or later. Stay safe."

"No promises."

#

A jug of oil sloshed under my arm. The clay pot warmed my side, still hot from its place beside my fireplace. Mama was supposed to use it in tonight's dinner. She had used it for Father's feast the other night—the one he never returned to.

Jurryt's house was within the main body of the town. His parents, both merchants, spent their livelihood on their home and products. Clothing tended to be an afterthought for them, as people so enveloped in their work. Jurryt himself was one of the rowdiest in his home, so perhaps he'd be more likely to join my cause.

I set the jug and candlesticks next to the front door. I couldn't let his mother assume they were gifts.

With the first knock, the door opened. His mother opened the door with a smile on her face. Her left hand rested on the edge of the door, ready to shut it at a moment's notice. "Minke, what are you doing here?"

Ah, the smile wasn't genuine. It took me a moment to discern it from our previous meetings. "I'm here to ask Jurryt if he wants to go and play in the forest."

"Why would he play with you? You're always making him do dangerous things," she said. "You even got your own father killed."

I swallowed.

"I grew up with your parents. They tried to hide the reason why your father's friend died. Why my brother died." The Laninga's son.

69

Mama's ex-fiancé. "You're not surprised." The corners of her eyes crinkled. "So they told you. Did they tell you that your father abandoned that boy as he cried out for help? He didn't die immediately. The deer wanted him to have a slow death."

Jurryt's mother leaned on the door frame when she spit onto the candlesticks. "You thought I wouldn't see them, even though this is my home. Minke, you have a lot to learn. Just make sure your brother doesn't end up a murderer like you and your father."

She shut the door in my face. I stood there for a moment, eyes focused on the worn wood. If Jurryt's parents were like this, then so would Achim's parents.

I was to kill the Horned Boy alone.

#

Through the bushes, I watched the Horned Boy's caramel pullover shift and strain. Snow drifted onto his bedhead of hair. I sunk deeper into a crouch as he laughed, sharing bites of pansies with his deer. The blood that stained their hooves and maws flaked off as he rubbed their faces. The attitude he held when I had come by days ago had to have been an act. Someone wouldn't act like this in front of carnivorous animals unless they truly felt at ease.

Some deer nuzzled his chest and back like dogs would. Others ran in circles around each other, wearing deep grooves into the snow. For the first time, I noticed the roots they lept over and the stump the Boy sat upon. The only tree to grow within the Treus House's perimeter, and it was dead.

I slunk backward, deeper into the forest. The fence surrounding the Treus House had been painted a red as vibrant as the blood of the massacre. Once it was hardly within sight, I began my circle around the House. The deer's sense of smell may be great, but it wasn't great enough to track me from twenty meters away.

Carefully and slowly, I started my short journey to the back of the property. Sticks littered the forest floor beneath the snow, so my stomach tensed with my every step. The brownish green of the House's cracked paint faded through the layers of tree and bush. The fence remained just as red. My boots crunched on powdered snow, inch by inch, foot by foot, until the behind of the House lingered within sight.

I braced myself at the fence, holding onto the wood with my left hand and the jar with my right. Ahead of me was the back of the Treus House. It was just as dilapidated as the front, but there was a door at floor level. I licked my finger and held it in the air.

One. Two. Three.

I shot off toward the backdoor. My feet crunched against the snow, but wind blew in my favor. Downwind in this weather, I ran as fast as I'd like while the Boy could never notice me.

The door handle rustled in my shaking fingers. Slipping off a glove, I opened the door and slipped inside, crossing several steps. Indoors was no warmer than outdoors. I set down the jar of oil. Before anything else, I had to return what I had stolen.

Upstairs remained as dirty as before, with no sign that the dust had been [moved]. The Boy never went inside. The bark was cracked when I fished it out of my pocket. From the second-to-the-top step, I chucked the bark across the hall. Nothing but the misfortune of my own creation.

I put my hands on my hips when I looked around the base floor and listened. The wind howled as violently as before through glassless windows. I crawled to one by the front porch. The Boy sat with his deer as calmly as before. His cheeks were pinker than the last time I was here. But he hadn't noticed me.

I used a ladle to pour a thin layer of oil by each wall. A shining path of oil crisscrossed the house, blocking each exit. A puddle shimmered in the center and dyed the floorboards a deep brown. From a canteen, I splattered water across the room.

With the jar against the front door, blocking entry, I crouched and set out my remaining materials. I stuck a metal rod against a small piece of flint until a spark shone and grew. The spark caught on a scrap fabric with an orange glow. The flame flickered as it jumped onto a candlestick. Yellow and blue.

I lit the second candlestick with the first and clutched them both in my right hand. This had to be the moment.

The sun crossed midday when at last I opened the front door. It slammed against the porch railing. With quick movements, I threw the remaining oil across the porch.

"Back again for more?" the Boy said. He caressed the muzzle of a fawn as he careened his neck to face me. Its wide eyes appeared sweet, but appearances were nothing more than lies when it came to the deer of Treus House. His eyes traced my figure from my fingers on the doorway to my boots to the burning candles in my hands. "You fool."

"That's right." I shifted my weight onto one leg and hid the candle from the wind with my hand. From this angle, the Horned Boy was welcome to the sight of flickering flames growing higher and higher. My hair waved behind me, growing closer and closer to the flames with each second.

For the first time, I saw the Horned Boy stand. His trousers were dusted with snow, same as his pullover, but he didn't shiver. His limbs were like those of a deer: long and slender. The power behind each stride was something ordinary people could only dream of.

His deer lunged and bared their teeth.

"Be careful, Boy. I'll drop it if you come closer." I lowered the candles as a warning.

The deer drew back as he came one step closer. "You smell of oil. If you're not careful, you'll burn down with the House." With my silence, he added, "You're making a mistake of yourself."

"Too late for you to show sympathy."

I showed my back to the Horned Boy when I tossed the candlesticks into the House as if I were skipping rocks. He could have me down within seconds if he wanted to, but that would put him within reach of the flames as they flared. Water and oil became a nasty combination when fire was added to the mix.

Wood creaked and gave way as the pool of liquid shot up into a bonfire. The heat spread throughout the lower floor, my face red with joy and warmth. Traces of the Treus House disappeared with each lick of flame.

I staggered back, dragging my feet to spread the oil further. A few more seconds and the floor inside should begin to give way. The doorway hid the staircase, so I hoped that the fire spread to the upper level soon enough. I wanted it to burn and the bark with it.

Cold fingers grabbed me by the nape of my neck and pulled me to the snowy ground several feet below me. A scream, but my lungs felt breathless. Had to be hooves.

I blinked away my shock and try to sit up, only to be pushed down by more cold hands and hooves. The Horned Boy kneeled on top of me with his hands against my shoulders. His inhuman strengthen turned my attempts into feeble movements. I coughed.

Small nips tore into my skin. Skin gave way to flesh. Flesh gave way to bone. I cried from the burning shock of my shinbone being revealed to the air.

The Boy looked at me with wet, warm eyes. They were green, no, brown. Hazel eyes. Those long eyelashes couldn't hide them when he looked down on me. His pink cheeks puffed up from the curl of his lips and the raising of his ears. Ah. Smiling.

"You never had a chance at winning this, child," he said. "Come nightfall, the House will be repaired."

Words lodged in my throat and mind. *How will you rebuild? Deer have hooves. You're one person. Let go of me. The purple-pink flames are so pretty.*

"Try again next time."

I relaxed into the warmth surrounding my body and the melted snow.

acknowledgments

I have myriad people to thank for how far I've come.

I'd like to thank my parents for their consistent support, love, and encouragement. They have always been there for me, even when I didn't realize it. Thank you, Ellen, for always being sweet to me. Your oatmeal was always nice to eat when I felt ill.

For those at SDSCPA, I'd like to say thank you to Mrs. Strasser and Mrs. Ten for all of the techniques they have taught me and the base they created for my writing voice to flourish. Thank you to Carmen, as well, for your amazing artwork and friendship.

I am thankful to have met Liv during the early stages of my high school years. We have been through a lot together, and since we're both writers, it has been nice to get to know her on various creative levels.

Those with the greatest influence on me since CSSSA have been Phinny Kiyomura and Katherine. Phinny forced me to go beyond what I thought I could do as a writer. Before, I never would have considered writing a whole movie in a day. Thank you to Katherine for encouraging me to develop my technical skills and have fun as a writer. Our creative partnership challenged me in countless ways I'll always be thankful for.

I have many of those at YoungArts to thank. The organization brought me together with Kaitlyn, Catherine, Kaya, Anna, Lily, and Shirley—all wonderful girls from various writing backgrounds. Seeing their growth over the past few years has been deeply motivating and inspiring. Thank you to Jasmine Bailey, Joan Morgan, Delali Ayivor, Mitzi Miller, d. Sabela Grimes, Selwyn Hinds, Adam Mansbach, and Andrea Assaf for your professional insight and mentorship. My week at UCLA with YoungArts pushed me outside my creative comfort zone by learning to read my writing aloud. For that, I'd like to thank Jayla for accompanying me through my piece and her creative insight.

Thank you, Susan DeFreitas, for being real with me about my novel. That feedback is priceless to me, and I still refer back to it even years later. You pinpointed my weaknesses in a way that has forced me to be aware of them with every word I type. Thank you, Josie, Odessa, Isabelle, and Isabelle for being a super fun writing group who gives great feedback and company.

During my junior year, I was a co-editor-in-chief with co-EIC Chelsea, visual editor Angel, assistant editor Tenza, and staffer Vaishnavi. You all made that magazine a lot of fun. At one point, I ended up looking forward to going in the tiny room with the Obama shrine three times a week. Tenza, you especially made my high school experience. Though I was afraid of you during freshman year, I don't know what experiencing all those classes would be like without you.

Lastly, I'd like to thank all my wonderful animals who have accompanied me over the years: Kai, Malik, Chica, Kavik, Athena, Teddy, Chewy, Marshmallow, Mimi, Greystripe, Bob, Vim, Bernie, Amber, Lucky, Lachlan, and Peanut. I wouldn't be the person I am today without you.

zahra linsky

Zahra Linsky was a creative writing major at the San Diego School of Creative and Performing Arts before moving onto becoming a chemistry and forensic science double-major at Cedar Crest College. During her time at SDSCPA, she was recognized for her writing by the National YoungArts Foundation and Scholastic Art and Writing.

She hopes to continue writing as a college student, while exploring her varying interests. Her favorite way to spend an afternoon is cuddling up with her dogs.